SUPER PIZZA & KID KALE

BY PHAEA CREDE

DRAWINGS BY ZACH SMITH

VIKING

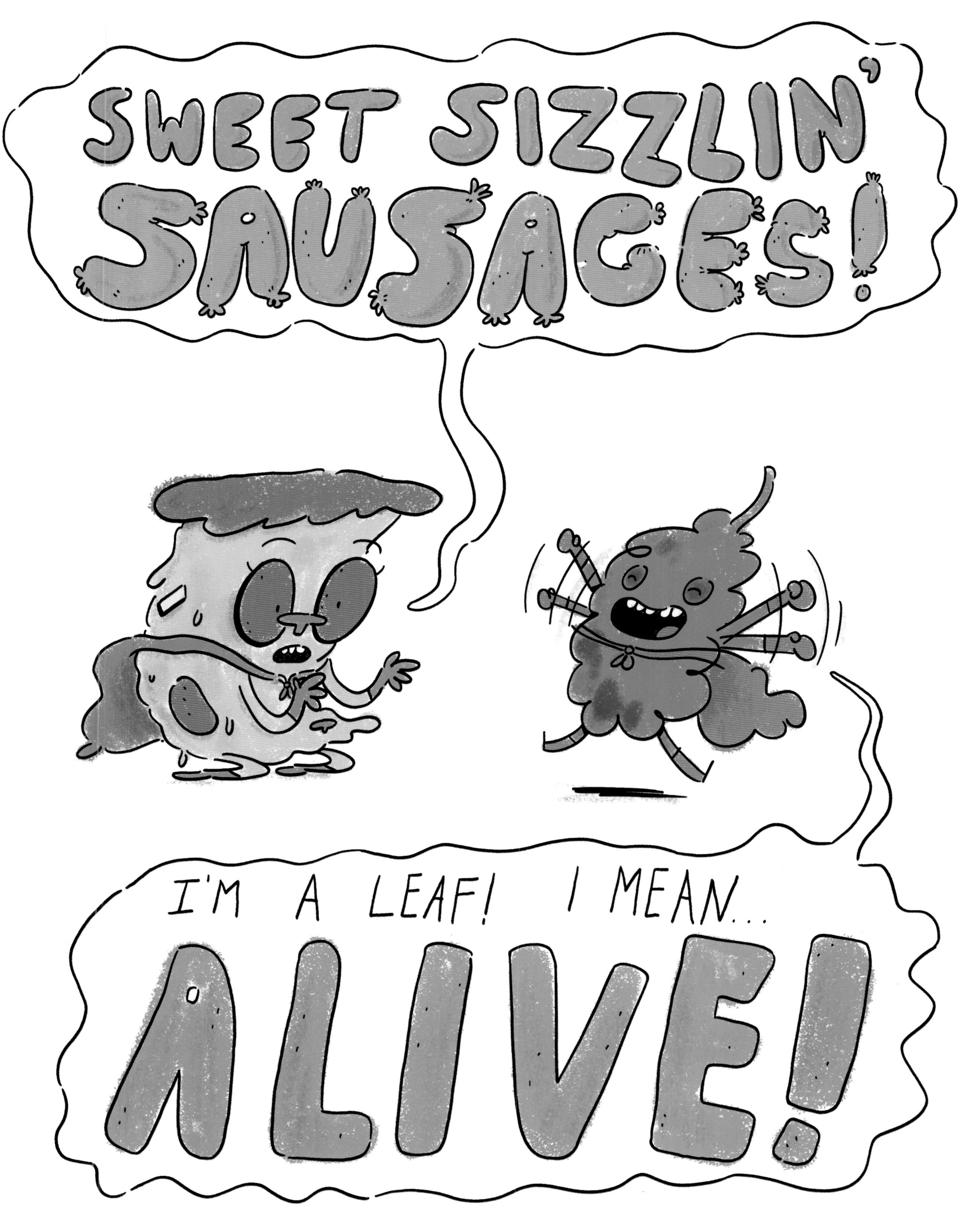
SWEET SIZZLIN' SAUSAGES!
I'M A LEAF! I MEAN... ALIVE!

Super Pizza and Kid Kale had been
as close as garlic and bread.

They lifted each other up.

They never let each other down.

And when it came to good ideas,
they were on the same plate:
WHAT IF WE USED OUR SUPERPOWERS...
TO BE HEROES!
bruce
juice
protein jr.
mystery gel

A wedge-shaped blur flew to her aid.
A parachute of produce brought her gently to the ground.

But something was off.

The fibrous fellow stewed as they flew away.

It wasn't.

Halting a book stack's topple . . .

only Super Pizza was slathered with praise.

Blocking a baseball most foul . . .

Kid Kale was left in the dust.

And mopping up a Meatloaf Monday mega-mess,
the marinara marvel ate up the attention . . .

while the tender green was left feeling shredded.

The wood-fired warrior scoffed.

Kid Kale didn't take kindly to this biting betrayal.

The once flavorful friendship had suddenly soured.

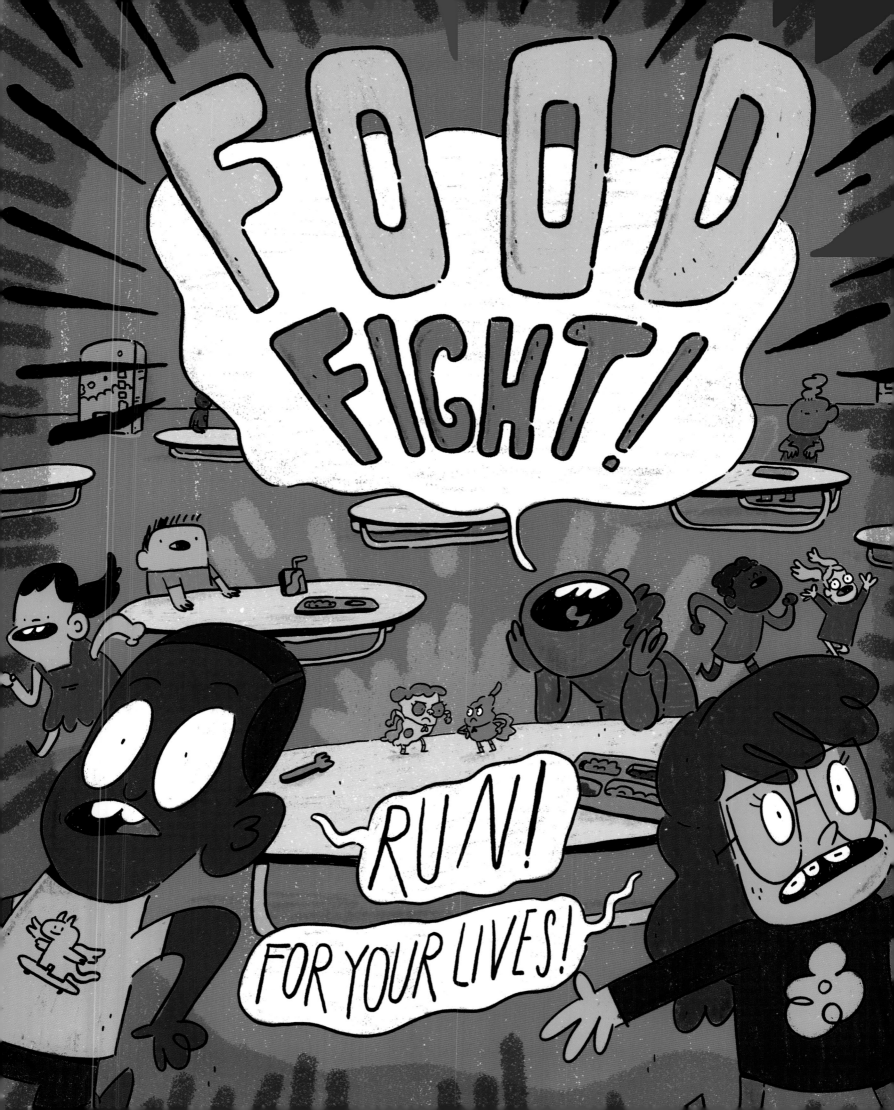

They hurled each other up.

They let each other down.

And when it came to bad ideas, they were on the same plate.

In a flash, Kid Kale's fury faded.

The dough-slinger gasped.

DON'T DREAD, FLATBREAD!
THUNK!
I HAVE A PLAN TO MAKE THINGS RIGHT.

The lean green roughage machine led their crustfallen comrade in an all-school cleanup.

Super Pizza smiled tenderly at their best frond.

Kid Kale grinned from curl to curl.

And off the combo flew, ready to right wrongs in thirty minutes . . . or less.

To Harvey, a super sidekick. —P. C.

To Landon & Bennett Turnwald
of Byron Center, Michigan. —Z. S.

VIKING
An imprint of Penguin Random House LLC, New York

First published in the United States of America by Viking,
an imprint of Penguin Random House LLC, 2022

Visit us online at penguinrandomhouse.com.

Library of Congress Cataloging-in-Publication Data is available.

Manufactured in China

ISBN 9780593403709

1 3 5 7 9 10 8 6 4 2

TOPL

Design by Lucia Baez · Text set in Minou

The art for this book was made digitally on an Apple iPad Pro with an Apple Pencil
and Procreate—usually while lying down on the floor.